18.95

Follett

3/3/04

A Teen
Eating Disorder
Prevention
Book

Understanding
Anorexia
Nervosa

Debbie Stanley

The Rosen Publishing Group, Inc./New York

Published in 1999 by The Rosen Publishing Group, Inc.
29 East 21st Street, New York, NY 10010

Library of Congress Cataloging-in-Publication Data

Stanley, Debbie.
    Understanding Anorexia nervosa / Debbie Stanley.
      p.   cm.
    Includes bibliographical references and index.
    Summary: Discusses the causes and consequences of anorexia nervosa, as well as ways to treat and prevent this condition.
    ISBN 0-8239-2877-2
    1. Anorexia nervosa — Juvenile literature. 2. Eating disorders — Juvenile literature. [1. Anorexia nervosa. 2. Eating disorders.] I. Title. II. Series.
RC552.A5S77   1999
616.85'27—dc21   99-15943
                                      CIP
                                      AC

Manufactured in the United States of America

ABOUT THE AUTHOR

Debbie Stanley has a bachelor's degree in journalism and a master's degree in industrial and organizational psychology.

Contents

Introduction

Marjorie's boyfriend doesn't understand her commitment to excellence. She works hard to get good grades, schedules time each day for exercise, and makes sure she gets enough sleep. She makes time to see him on Saturday nights, but other than that, her time is consumed with homework, exercise, and chores. Marjorie's friends think she's obsessed with getting things done and needs to take time to just do nothing, but the idea of wasting time is appalling to Marjorie. Her boyfriend's friends think she's a control freak and give him a hard time for staying with her when he could be with someone fun.

Weight is the topic of discussion every time Jessica and her friends get together. They know all about eating disorders. "Everyone keeps saying they're bad for you, but we want to be skinny, so we help each other stay committed to

1

not eating," Jessica says. "We watch out for each other. We'll make sure that none of us gets too skinny or sick from it or anything."

When classes started in the fall, Stefan noticed that Louise, his lab partner in chemistry, was pretty and slim, but rather quiet and reserved. When he asked her to sit with him at lunch, she snubbed him—she mumbled something about having to work in the library— and disappeared into the stream of kids changing classes. But when he went to the library at lunchtime that day, she wasn't there. And he's never seen her in the cafeteria, either. Stefan's friends have a running bet on whether anyone can get Louise to eat something; they taunt her with candy bars, bags of chips, and cookies while she's at her locker, but no one has ever been able to convince her to take a bite. Stefan figures it's all part of her snobbish personality: "People who starve themselves are so stupid and self-absorbed. They're just trying to get attention."

These are just a few examples of the attitudes some people have about anorexia nervosa, the deadliest of all eating disorders. Some people falsely believe that being anorexic is something to be proud of, that it shows willpower, that it is a conscious choice, or that it is an attention-getting ploy. This misinformation leads to a lot of pain for the sufferer and her friends and family.

The truth is that anorexia nervosa is a serious disease that kills 10 percent of its victims and

> **Note:** Because an estimated 90 to 95 percent of people suffering from anorexia are female, the feminine pronouns ("she" and "her") are used throughout the book instead of "he or she" or "him/her." This is for the sake of clarity and simplicity and is not intended to exclude males, who represent a small but nonetheless real and important segment of anorexics. Boys and young men as well as girls and young women are encouraged to educate themselves about the risk factors and warning signs associated with the disease and to learn how they can help themselves and their friends.

leaves many more with permanent physical damage. It is not a diet, a fad, or a "phase that she's going through."

This book is intended to help you:

- ⊙ sift through the mountain of misinformation surrounding eating disorders and learn the facts about anorexia

- ⊙ become familiar with its symptoms and the warning signs that accompany it

- ⊙ know where to begin in seeking help for yourself or a friend or family member

⊙ recognize the role society plays in the existence of anorexia and what you can do to make a positive impact on our culture's attitudes about eating disorders

⊙ begin to think about healthy ways to keep control of your life and your well-being.

Anorexia: Facts and Myths

Anorexia nervosa, most often called anorexia, is an emotional disorder with physical symptoms. While most emotional or mental illnesses are not easy to detect simply by looking at the sufferer, anorexia's symptoms are obvious: Victims of late-stage anorexia appear grotesquely thin to others, even though they believe themselves to be fat.

DISORDERED EATING

Anorexia and bulimia nervosa, the condition characterized by cycles of bingeing (eating a large amount of food at one time) and purging (vomiting or using laxatives to get rid of the binged food), have long been considered "eating disorders." New thinking in this area, however, has led to the concept of "disordered eating," which is much more comprehensive. The difference in wording is subtle but important. "In the past, an 'eating disorder' was defined as either anorexia nervosa or bulimia nervosa," Dr. Aurelia

5

Nattiv and Linda Lynch reported in the journal *Physician and Sportsmedicine.* "The new concept of 'disordered eating' emphasizes the spectrum of abnormal eating behavior, with poor nutritional habits on one end, and anorexia and bulimia on the other."

This broadening of the scope of potential problem areas has allowed doctors, coaches, and counselors to see other seemingly less dangerous conditions that could lead to the extremes of anorexia or bulimia. It also allows people to recognize that poor eating habits need not be as critical as persistent anorexia or bulimia to be serious and worthy of attention.

In her book *Lost for Words: The Psychoanalysis of Anorexia and Bulimia,* Em Farrell estimates that an incredible 80 percent of all people are believed to be affected by borderline disordered eating, known technically as sub-clinical eating disorder. That means only 20 percent of all people, or just one in five, have a healthy attitude toward food.

CONSEQUENCES OF DISORDERED EATING

Anorexia and bulimia are technically mental disorders, but their consequences are physical. The mental illnesses known as "eating disorders" are responsible for more deaths than any other psychiatric condition. The National Institute of Mental Health (NIMH) reports that one in ten anorexics die from the condition, either from starvation, from complications such as heart attacks, or from suicide. The overall mortality rate for eating disorder sufferers who do not receive treatment is estimated at 10 to 20 percent.

Sufferers are usually adolescent girls and young women between the ages of twelve and twenty-five, although both diseases are becoming more common in younger girls and may begin or persist well into adulthood. A growing body of research indicates that the number of male victims is also increasing, but current estimates are that between 90 and 95 percent of eating disorder sufferers are female.

Formal diagnosis of anorexia and bulimia is made based on a set of criteria in the *Diagnostic and Statistical Manual of Mental Disorders* (DSM), a guidebook used by mental health professionals. To be considered anorexic according to the DSM, a person must be at least 15 percent lighter than the minimum body weight for her height; to be diagnosed a bulimic, she must average at least two binge-and-purge sessions per week for at least three months. In addition to these factors, other conditions concerning the victim's self-image and attitude toward food must exist. According to these guidelines, an estimated 1 percent of girls and young women are anorexic, and another 2 to 3 percent are bulimic. Also, it is not uncommon for a person to have both anorexia and bulimia: She will either progress from one to the other or alternate between the two.

Beyond the relatively small percentages mentioned above, it is important to point out that many more people are currently struggling with disordered eating. Even if they do not yet fit the textbook definition of anorexia or bulimia, they are suffering the physical, mental, and emotional consequences of these diseases.

The American Anorexia/Bulimia Association (AABA) reports that approximately 15 percent of young women have "substantially disordered eating attitudes and behaviors" and more than five million Americans are struggling with eating disorders. Of that number, some are anorexic, while others are bulimic or suffer from binge eating disorder (BED). Beyond the three most serious eating disorders, however, are a number of other conditions, including compulsive exercise, malnutrition, fad or yo-yo dieting, smoking, alcohol and drug abuse, depression, and even self-mutilation and obsessive-compulsive disorder (OCD), which are correlated in varying degrees with disordered eating.

MYTH VERSUS FACT

Anorexia is the most well-known and widely discussed of all eating disorders. Chances are you have heard quite a bit about it, from friends, parents, teachers, coaches, doctors, and the media. Unfortunately, some of that information is probably false. Below are some common myths about anorexia and the facts that prove them wrong.

Myth: People with anorexia are self-centered and vain. **Fact:** Anyone can seem stuck-up, but the truth is that people with eating disorders have low self-esteem. Far from being happy with or proud of their appearance, anorexics hate the way they look and believe that losing weight will help. Even when they have lost a large amount of weight and have become dangerously thin, anorexics still see themselves as fat. They base their self-worth on their ability to control their eating, but in doing so they set themselves up for disappointment because their rigid rules are impossible to follow.

Myth: Only girls get anorexia.
Fact: While the vast majority of eating disorder sufferers are female, the number of male sufferers is steadily increasing. Some researchers believe that there are more male victims than anyone knows about, because eating disorders are seen as a girl's problem, and boys are reluctant to admit to having them or to seek help.

Myth: Anorexia is just stubbornness and defiance.
Fact: This myth is especially common among parents, who see their child's refusal to eat as a discipline problem. It is true that anorexics are attempting to take control, but not in the way their parents might think. Anorexics feel that their lives are out of control, and they seek comfort by taking charge of their eating. Sometimes it's the only thing in their lives that they can have any control over.

Myth: Anorexia victims are abused at home.
Fact: Unfortunately, some anorexia victims are also victims of physical, psychological, or sexual abuse. There are no conclusive studies to prove that abuse causes anorexia, or that a larger percentage of abused kids are also anorexic, but researchers have found that an unstable home environment is often the trigger for an eating disorder. This could mean that the victim's parents are getting a divorce, another child in the family is seriously ill, or the family is having financial problems.

It could even mean that some happy event—a sibling's marriage or move to college—is bringing about changes in the family. Therefore, it is possible that an anorexia victim is being abused, and it is likely that there is some sort of change going on in the family, but it is not at all correct to assume that all anorexics are abused.

Myth: Anorexia is a good way to lose weight if you know when to stop.
Fact: Anorexia is an incredibly dangerous way to diet. It is extremely unhealthy and kills approximately one in ten of its victims. Unfortunately, most anorexics started out trying to lose just a few pounds, but could not stop themselves from trying to lose more. Anorexia is not a simple weight-loss technique; it is an emotional illness that leaves its victims powerless to stop it.

Myth: The physical effects of anorexia are reversible.
Fact: Much of the damage anorexia inflicts on the body cannot be repaired. Victims who survive anorexia may be left with permanent complications and damage to their hearts, digestive and reproductive systems, and bones.

Anorexia affects all the systems of the body. It slows digestion, which causes constipation. It makes you feel constantly cold and causes a thin layer of hair, called lanugo, to grow all over your body. If you are female, it stops your period. Anorexia causes you to be weak and tired constantly; many anorexics faint just about every day. Anorexia also gives you a pasty complexion and makes your hair fall out, and brings on all kinds of side effects that are caused by a lack of certain vitamins and minerals. Your palms and the soles of your feet may turn yellow, and you may begin to bruise or bleed easily.

As the disease progresses, your body begins to break down muscle tissue to survive. This leads to liver and kidney damage, and eventually kidney failure, which can kill you or leave you dependent on dialysis for the rest of your life. If you are female, you may develop osteoporosis, which weakens your bones and makes them break easily. Both males and females may be made infertile, or unable to have children, by the effects of the disease. Your heart is also affected by the mineral imbalance brought on by anorexia; many victims die of cardiac arrest.

Myth: People with anorexia are insane.
Fact: Anorexics suffer from an emotional illness. This is not the same as being insane. However, this myth is common because anorexics have such a skewed body image and obsession with food issues that their thinking and behavior seem strange to others. Also, anorexics are sometimes admitted to a hospital for treatment, which leads some people to the inaccurate assumption that the victim has been committed to a mental institution.

Myth: Anorexics never eat anything.
Fact: Most anorexics did not simply stop eating one day. While a person may go several days, or, in extreme cases, even weeks without eating, most do eat small amounts of food, such as some lettuce or

a few celery sticks. Their food intake drops gradually from normal amounts to slightly inadequate amounts, and finally to much less than subsistence level. Most victims of anorexia have also fought one or more other eating disorders in the past, and sometimes they show symptoms of more than one at the same time. For example, people suffering from bulimia, the eating disorder characterized by cycles of binge eating and purging, may progress to anorexia without treatment. Some people alternate between bulimia and anorexia.

Myth: Anorexics can't stand the sight of food.
Fact: Many anorexics enjoy cooking. They may collect recipes, spend hours in the kitchen preparing gourmet meals for their families, and take great pleasure in watching others enjoy food. Anorexics are constantly hungry, and some find that watching others eat makes their feelings of deprivation more bearable. Preparing food for others also serves as a distraction from the fact that the anorexic is not eating.

Myth: If you're diagnosed with anorexia, they put you in the hospital for a long time and force you to eat.
Fact: Some people in the most advanced stages of anorexia must be closely monitored in a hospital, sometimes against their will, to keep them from starving themselves to death. However, there are many other less extreme treatment options available. The level of treatment needed depends on the severity of the victim's condition and on her willingness to cooperate with the treatment program.

Myth: Anorexics are too tired to exercise, so athletes can't be anorexic.

Fact: Anorexia does sap a person's strength; victims often feel tired, dizzy, or light-headed, because they aren't consuming enough calories or liquids to keep their energy levels up. However, many anorexics use exercise as a way to speed up their weight loss, and they will continue to exercise through the pain and fatigue, sometimes even until they faint or collapse. There are many athletes who suffer from eating disorders, and in some cases females develop another serious condition known as the Female Athlete Triad, which is the combination of disordered eating, osteoporosis (softening of the bones), and amenorrhea (loss of monthly periods).

Now that you've learned the truth behind many of the myths of anorexia, read on for more information on anorexia and other eating disorders, their causes, and ways to avoid them or find help in overcoming them.

2 Other Eating Disorders and Related Conditions

In the previous chapter, you learned the facts about anorexia nervosa, and you also learned that there are a number of other serious conditions that may share symptoms with anorexia or even exist at the same time in the same person. These conditions include bulimia nervosa, binge eating disorder (BED), compulsive exercise, malnutrition, smoking and substance abuse, depression, self-mutilation, and obsessive-compulsive disorder (OCD).

BULIMIA NERVOSA

Sara: "I hate getting up in the morning, and I hate lunch break, and I hate getting out of school. Any time I have to be alone with myself I hate it, because then I eat and eat and eat. Then I feel so horrible about what I ate and so scared that I'm going to gain weight, I run to the nearest bathroom and throw it all back up."

Bulimia is characterized by alternating episodes of binge eating and purging. A binge may be anything from a bag of chips to a whole bag of groceries, but what every binge has in common is that the sufferer feels out of control and unable to stop eating. The binge stops only when the person is physically unable to eat any more or when her feelings of guilt and self-loathing become so strong that the desire to purge takes over.

Purging most often takes the form of vomiting; the bulimic makes herself throw up in a desperate attempt to get rid of the food consumed during the binge. While some people stick their fingers down their throats to make themselves vomit, others use dangerous drugs intended only to induce vomiting after the accidental ingestion of poison. Some people also abuse laxatives or overexercise to keep themselves from gaining weight after a binge. In addition to bingeing and purging, some bulimics periodically deny themselves food for a day or more, much like anorexics do.

BINGE EATING DISORDER (BED)

Michele: "You know how there are some people who can't eat if they're upset, and some people who can't do anything but eat if they're upset? Well, I'm the second type. And I'm always upset about something."

Binge eating disorder is similar to bulimia in that the person is unable to stop herself from consuming large amounts of food at one time. But unlike bulimia, the person does not purge the food.

As a result, many people suffering from BED, also known as compulsive eating, are overweight or obese. An estimated 30 percent of people participating in medically supervised weight control programs are found to be suffering from BED, compared to an average of 2 percent of the population overall.

Like anorexia and bulimia, BED is more common among females than males; approximately 60 percent of its victims are female. This is significantly different from the other eating disorders, however, in which men represent a much smaller percentage of victims. BED sufferers feel overwhelming shame at being unable to control their eating, and are also likely to have low self-esteem or suffer from depression. It is important to recognize that the inability to keep from overeating is not just gluttony or laziness—it is a disease, and its sufferers, like those of any other disease, need help to overcome it.

COMPULSIVE EXERCISE

Sue: "I love the way I feel after a good, hard workout—like I've really accomplished something, and my body will take care of itself for the next twenty-four hours. When I miss a workout, I get panicky. I start to worry that my health is going to break down, that I'll start gaining weight, and I won't be able to stop it. If I miss a workout one day, I don't eat that day."

Compulsive exercise has long been considered a side effect of anorexia or bulimia, but researchers are now beginning to think of it as a separate problem that may occur on its own and often

YES, YOU CAN HAVE BOTH ANOREXIA AND BULIMIA

As research continues into eating disorders, more is being learned about the co-existence of both anorexia and bulimia in the same victim. Experts used to believe that a person could have just one of the two diseases, but now more evidence for the existence of "bulimarexia" or "anorexia/bulimia" is being found. The condition usually manifests itself in alternating cycles of starvation and bingeing/purging.

Some experts believe the combination of anorexia and bulimia is even more dangerous to the victim than having just one or the other disease, because each damages the body in certain ways: Combining the damage of both may be even more deadly than anorexia's one-in-ten fatality rate.

Perhaps the most well-known victim of anorexia/bulimia is singer and musician Karen Carpenter, who died in 1983 of a heart attack brought on by her struggle with eating disorders. Like many bulimics, she had abused ipecac syrup to induce vomiting, and became progressively thinner and weaker before beginning treatment. Ironically, she seemed to be on the road to recovery when she died; despite her efforts to help herself, her body was simply too damaged to go on.

accompanies another eating disorder. Since everyone knows that exercise burns calories, it makes sense that people who are obsessed with thinness would use exercise to lose weight. But how can you tell whether your exercise regimen is healthy or compulsive?

If you exercise regularly or participate in a sport, ask yourself why you do it. Is it because you enjoy the activity, or because you like to win, or because you know that exercise is an important component of overall health? Or is there more to it than that? If you quit your team or skipped your workouts for a while, how would you feel about yourself?

If your self-esteem is based largely on your performance in a sport or in your ability to stick to a workout regimen, you may be headed for a problem with exercise compulsion.

OTHER CONDITIONS RELATED TO ANOREXIA

Malnutrition

Dara: "I eat sweets all the time. Whenever there's cake in the house, I have it for breakfast. When I get home from school, I have something salty or crunchy or cheesy with a bottle of pop, and then I have ice cream and cake, or some sort of candy. I know you're supposed to eat fruits and vegetables, but I don't like them, and my parents don't either, so they don't force me to eat them."

Most people think of malnutrition as a chronic condition affecting only poverty-stricken children in other countries, where there isn't enough food or water. The fact is that malnutrition exists in America, even among people who can have all the food they want. In cases of child abuse and neglect, it is not uncommon to find that the victims have not been fed properly. They may be low on certain vitamins and minerals, or they may be so starved that their bellies are swollen like those of the children in the pictures we all see from impoverished Third World countries. However, many children with loving parents are lacking in vitamins and minerals crucial for health and growth, including calcium and iron. The cause of this is poor eating habits.

A child who always drinks pop instead of milk will almost certainly develop a calcium deficiency. A child, especially a girl, who does not eat meat but is not taught how to get the iron she needs from other food sources will probably become anemic. These are common, completely preventable forms of malnutrition in this country. Among older children and even adults, fad dieting can also lead to malnutrition. Any diet that severely limits or forbids the consumption of an entire food group, such as carbohydrates or fats, puts the dieter in danger of missing out on important nutrients, either because they are found mostly in the forbidden foods, or because they come from allowable foods but cannot be absorbed by the body without the help of the forbidden foods.

Besides depriving your body of important nutrients, which in some cases cannot be replaced simply by taking a daily multivitamin, limiting yourself to a strict diet regimen that does not include any of your favorite foods can backfire. The lack of certain foods, such as fats, combined with the psychological strain of harsh dieting, can bring on a binge in which you "lose control" and eat everything you've been forcing yourself to avoid. The subsequent guilt that you feel after the binge then prompts you to go back on the same, or an even stricter, diet. This cycle of impossible dieting and loss of control is called "yo-yo dieting," and it is bad for your health. Besides putting you at risk for malnutrition, it could lead to an eating disorder.

It is important that every child learn about the body's nutritional requirements and think about them with every meal and snack. A child who understands that drinking pop, eating candy, skipping meals, or avoiding entire food groups all the time is damaging to her health will be more likely to make better choices. If you recognize these or similar poor eating habits in yourself, do some research on nutrition and begin to make healthy changes in the way you eat. If you don't get well-balanced meals at home, list some healthy meals and foods and ask the person who prepares your meals to make them for you. It is never too late to learn about nutrition and to begin to provide your body with the proper fuel.

Smoking and Substance Abuse

Kylie: "My parents really gave me hell when they first caught me smoking. I knew they would, but I figure they've got no right to talk, because they both smoke like chimneys."

Bev: "My dad loves his beer. Since I was little, he's let me have some. I guess he thought

IS IT HEALTHY TO BE A VEGETARIAN?

There is one diet variation that eliminates food categories but can be followed in a healthy manner: vegetarianism.

Being a vegetarian simply means not eating meat, but there are actually quite a number of variations on vegetarianism. Some people only eliminate beef or other red meats from their diets; others avoid all animal products, including beef, chicken, pork, fish, and even eggs and dairy products such as milk, cheese, and yogurt.

A person's reason for choosing a vegetarian diet may include religious or political beliefs that forbid eating another creature, or health considerations linked to allergies or animal fats. If you are a vegetarian, it is possible for you to fulfill your nutritional needs, but it takes some education, planning, and effort. If you choose a vegetarian lifestyle, make sure you educate yourself and are committed to it for healthy reasons, not for weight loss or because your friends are doing it.

it was cute to see a little kid sipping beer. Sometimes he gives it to the dog, too. But now that I'm older, I really have a taste for it, and I wonder how cute he'll think it is when he finds out I'm the one drinking all his beer, not his brother who lives with us."

Lyssa: "I started smoking pot when I first ran away. My parents brought me back, and they cried and said they would try to do better with me, but things didn't really change. It's easier to tolerate now though, because I can just get high and forget about it."

Any foreign substance that you put into your body alters it in some way. Tobacco, alcohol, and all drugs and supplements have various effects on your brain, heart, lungs, kidneys, liver, or other organs, and also on your body's respiratory, circulatory, endocrine, and digestive systems. Medications are used to make you better if you are sick by bringing on good changes in your body's organs and systems; supplements are intended to help your body reach its highest health potential. You have probably heard about the negative effects that smoking, drinking, and using drugs can have on your body, but did you know that they can also contribute to disordered eating?

Many people believe that smoking can keep you from gaining weight, so many girls use cigarettes as a dieting tool. This is extremely dangerous to your health, and it doesn't even work! The reason some people lose weight when they start smoking is that they tend to replace snacks with cigarettes. The reason some people gain weight when they quit smoking is just the opposite: Instead of "consuming" a cigarette, they reach for a snack.

Try to teach yourself to find something else to do with your hands and mouth instead of smoking or overeating—for example, begin a hobby such as singing or drawing. Get involved in an activity that you can't do while smoking or eating, such as a sport. That way, you can avoid two health risks, smoking and overeating, at the same time.

Drinking alcohol lowers your inhibitions and your ability to make good choices. Alcoholic beverages contain a lot of calories on their own, and when people drink, they also tend to eat more than normal. So, besides being dangerous to your health and your safety, not to mention illegal if you're underage, drinking can lead to binge eating. Drinking can also lead to malnutrition if it becomes the chronic and persistent condition known as alcoholism.

Many drugs have some of the same effects as alcohol: They lower your inhibitions, make you feel super-confident or invincible, or make you forget all the reasons you have for trying to eat healthy foods. Some drugs also increase or decrease your appetite. Laxatives, which are supposed to be used when you have constipation and can't have a bowel movement, and diuretics, which force your body to rid itself of water, are both commonly abused by people with eating disorders. Syrup of ipecac, which is intended to be used only to induce vomiting in people who have ingested poisons, is a poison itself and can cause death when misused.

The use of any drug for a purpose other than the one listed on the label can be extremely dangerous. No drug should be used to lose weight or to purge excess calories. The only exception to this rule is the use of a prescription drug, prescribed to you (not to a friend or parent) by a doctor and to be used under that doctor's close supervision. Even then, drug use should be a last resort for treating a dangerously obese person; a good, responsible doctor will never prescribe a weight-loss drug to a child or teen who simply wants to look better.

Of course, in many cases the use of tobacco, alcohol, or drugs points to a problem more severe than disordered eating. If you are currently using any of these substances, please stop trying to convince yourself that you can handle it, that it's no big deal, that everyone is doing it, or that it won't hurt you. The truth is that it is a big deal; it will hurt you and possibly kill you. Please find someone who can help you stop. There are groups (listed in the Where to Go for Help section at the end of this book) that exist to help with any problem, not just eating disorders.

Depression

Cherie: "I'm tired all the time. I just want to sleep. Sometimes I get frustrated with my homework, and I just go to bed. I sleep in late on the weekends, too—usually till 2 or 3 PM. There's just nothing interesting to do. My parents made me go to the doctor, and she said there's nothing wrong with me that would make me so tired. Maybe I'm just depressed."

Most people who suffer from eating disorders may also suffer from depression. Defined as an emotional condition characterized by feelings of hopelessness, inadequacy, or self-hatred, depression can be caused by any number of things or by nothing specific. Some people are prone to depression because of a chemical imbalance in their brains. Other people become depressed as a result of a crisis or sad occurrence in their lives or because they feel more and more unable to cope with everyday life.

Depression does not cause eating disorders, and eating disorders do not cause depression; instead, the circumstances in a person's life that cause one condition can also cause the other. When they occur together, both conditions must be treated to bring the sufferer back to a healthy, functional state. The health professional treating a victim of an eating disorder, or depression, or both, may prescribe an antidepressant medication to assist the sufferer in regaining psychological control and equilibrium. When that is accomplished, the person is better able to learn what she needs to change in her life to bring about recovery. It is important to realize that an antidepressant is not a cure; it simply reduces or eliminates the symptoms of depression and allows the sufferer to work on changing the things that brought it on in the first place.

Self-Mutilation

Evie: "Sometimes life just gets to be too much and the only thing that makes me feel better is

cutting myself. I take my time with it so it will
last. Sometimes I pull out my eyelashes too, and
I chew on my hair. I haven't been able to do that
last one lately, though—none of it is long
enough to reach my mouth any more."

Some people act on their feelings of self-hatred
by actually injuring themselves. But unlike the
anorexic, who injures her body by depriving it of
nutrients and straining its organs and systems, a
person who practices self-mutilation cuts her
body with a knife or razor blade, burns herself,
pulls out her hair, eyelashes, or eyebrows, or
does something else to cause herself pain. She
does not consciously intend to commit suicide;
instead, her goal is to replace her emotional pain
with more tolerable physical pain, to break
through her emotional numbness and allow herself to feel something, or to express anger or
other painful feelings.

People who practice self-mutilation are also
often suffering from an eating disorder. The thing
that self-mutilators have in common with anorexics,
bulimics, binge eaters, alcoholics, and drug abusers
is that they are attempting to rid themselves of psychological pain.

Obsessive/Compulsive Disorder (OCD)

Lanita: "I go to bed before my mom, but I
can't go to sleep until I hear her go into her
room. Then I get up and check the locks on
all the doors and windows, and I make sure
the alarm is set. Sometimes I can sleep after

that, but sometimes I lie awake worrying about the windows in her room, because I can't check those. And if I hear a noise, I have to go do it all over again or I will just lose my mind worrying."

Obsessive/compulsive disorder, or OCD, is a serious psychological condition characterized by rigid adherence to rituals such as checking door locks ten times each night, or washing your hands after touching anything or anyone (sometimes dozens of times each day). Jack Nicholson's character in the movie *As Good As It Gets* suffered from OCD; he had rituals for locking doors, putting on his shoes, washing his hands, avoiding sidewalk cracks, and many other common elements of daily life. When he was forced to deviate from these rituals, he experienced great psychological distress—fear, confusion, and a desperation to return his life to "normal."

Rituals are also common among eating disorder sufferers. Something as simple as refusing to eat any food that has touched another food on your plate, or insisting on eating one food at a time in a particular order (for example, the potatoes first, then the meat, then the vegetable) may signal an unhealthy preoccupation with eating. Such rituals do not automatically indicate that the person who follows them is suffering from OCD, but it could mean that the person has an underlying problem which is causing her to seek comfort in rigidly prescribed routines.

So, as you can see, there are a number of conditions that can exist along with an eating disorder, or in some cases may be mistaken for one. If you suspect you may have any of these conditions, or if you see signs in a friend, please seek help. The section entitled Where to Go for Help at the end of this book contains many helpful resources.

3 Who Has Anorexia?

The typical anorexic is a white female, approximately 15 to 25 percent below her ideal weight, and between the ages of twelve and eighteen. Anorexia rarely starts after age twenty-five. The American Anorexia/Bulimia Association (AABA) reports that 5 percent of adolescent and adult women have anorexia, bulimia, or binge eating disorder.

It is hypothesized that the vast majority of eating disorder sufferers are female, because society places a much greater burden of physical appearance on women than it does on men. It is estimated that one of every 250 girls between the ages of twelve and eighteen has struggled with an eating disorder at some time, but it is impossible to know for sure because not everyone asks for or receives help, and doctors are not required to report the number of eating disorder cases they treat.

VICTIM PROFILE: BALLERINA HEIDI GUENTHER

Twenty-two-year-old Heidi died in 1997 from complications arising from her eating disorder. A well-known dancer with the Boston Ballet, she was five feet, three inches tall and under ninety-three pounds when she died. Unfortunately, unrealistic size and weight requirements are common in the dance world; girls are expected to be more than just thin, but far below the recommendations of the standard height and weight charts. In her article "Eating Disorders," published on-line by Suite101.com, Heather Mudgett reports that actress Lea Thompson, star of the TV show *Caroline in the City*, was previously a dancer and was once rejected by a ballet company: "At 5'5" and 96 lbs., she was too 'stocky' to be considered."

DOES ANOREXIA AFFECT ONLY WHITE AMERICANS?

Eating disorders were long believed to challenge only white girls and young women, and some researchers speculate that, in the past, cultural differences did indeed protect black, Latina, Asian, and Native American females from anorexia and bulimia. Now, however, greater numbers of non-white females are coming forward to find help for disordered eating. No conclusions have yet been reached about whether this trend indicates an actual rise in eating disorders among non-white women or simply an increase in the reporting of them. What is certain, however, is that non-white women are no longer being ignored as at-risk for eating disorders. Conscientious scientists and doctors recognize that all girls and young women, regardless of race, are in danger of developing disordered eating habits as a result of the same societal pressures.

While the United States reports one of the highest rates of disordered eating in the world, other countries are not immune to the problem. Japan and China have seen a rise in anorexia and bulimia, but the shame associated with psychotherapy in those countries prevents many women from seeking treatment. Accurate measurement or even estimation of the extent of the problem there is impossible. Argentina's incidents of both conditions are three times as high as in the United States; the crisis of disordered eating in that country is attributed to a societal obsession with physical perfection that is even worse than ours.

WHAT ABOUT GUYS?

It is estimated that boys and men make up only 5 to 10 percent of all eating disorder sufferers. Approximately one million males, or 1 percent of the population, have anorexia, bulimia, or binge eating disorder, according to the AABA. The number of reported cases is growing, however, as men learn that eating disorders are not just "women's diseases."

Many men, especially heterosexuals, are still reluctant to seek help for anorexia or bulimia because in recent years the number of homosexual men seeking help for disordered eating has increased. It seems that many straight men are embarrassed to admit the problem. They are afraid that if they seek help, people will think they are gay. In reality, there is no known correlation between sexual preference and risk of disordered eating; being gay doesn't cause anorexia or bulimia, and having an eating disorder can't make anyone "turn gay." The higher reporting rate among gay men probably indicates that they are more willing to request help, not that more gays than straights are eating disorder sufferers.

Some preliminary research indicates that men may be more at risk than women for another problem that is similar to bulimia: binge eating disorder (BED), also known as compulsive eating. In our culture, men are expected to have a "healthy appetite," so when a boy eats an entire pizza by himself in one sitting, few people see it as a warning sign. If a girl were to do that, however, it would be much more likely to raise a red flag. While the girl would probably be embarrassed and ashamed, the boy would be inclined to brag about his feat.

WHAT ABOUT ABUSED KIDS?

Being trapped in an abusive or neglectful environment can certainly trigger disordered eating. However, researchers have not found a cause-and-effect relationship between child abuse and eating disorders in the victim. This means that children who suffer physical, emotional, or sexual abuse may be more vulnerable to disordered eating, in the same way that any child in a dangerous, unstable, or explosive environment is vulnerable. Researchers have not demonstrated, however, that abused children are in any more danger of becoming anorexic or bulimic than anyone else solely because of the abuse.

MOST AT RISK: YOUNG WOMEN AND THE FEMALE ATHLETE TRIAD

There is growing concern among those who work with female athletes over a set of three conditions now known as the Female Athlete Triad. Consisting of amenorrhea (the loss of one's monthly period), disordered eating, and osteoporosis (loss of density and increased brittleness of the bones), the condition is extremely dangerous and potentially fatal—and alarmingly common.

While an estimated 1 percent of the female population is considered anorexic and another 2 to 3 percent are bulimic, various studies have found that anywhere from 15 to 70 percent of female athletes practice pathogenic, or disease-causing, weight-control behaviors, which in some cases include anorexia and/or bulimia. Nattiv and Lynch emphasized in their essay for *Physician and Sportsmedicine,* "Although they may not fit the . . . criteria for anorexia or bulimia, they are still at risk for developing serious psychiatric, endocrine, and skeletal problems."

Approximately 2 to 5 percent of women in the general population have amenorrhea, but its prevalence among female athletes is estimated at anywhere from 3.4 percent to 66 percent, depending on the study's definition of the condition and the characteristics of its subject group. While there are many possible causes for amenorrhea (including the most obvious—pregnancy), in a female athlete the condition should alert the young woman's doctor or coach to evaluate her closely for disordered eating and osteoporosis.

Even if the other elements of the triad can be ruled out, amenorrhea should not be considered "normal" and allowed to continue without a thorough search for its cause. It once was believed that simply dipping below a certain percentage of body fat could cause a young woman's periods to stop even if she was otherwise fit and healthy. Therefore, it was not considered serious. Further research shows that the situation is not that simple. It is important to understand that amenorrhea is not healthy, even though the young woman experiencing it may welcome the convenience of not having a period each month and may even believe, falsely, that losing her period is a point of pride and indicates overall fitness.

Most people who hear the term "osteoporosis" think of very old women with hunched backs, weak joints, and bones that break with just one fall. Young women do not consider themselves at risk for the condition, and in fact, it is not common for a normal

VICTIM PROFILE: GYMNAST CHRISTY HENRICH

Christy was a world-class gymnast who died of multiple organ failure in 1994 as a result of her ongoing struggle with anorexia and bulimia. It has been reported that a U.S. gymnastics judge told the teenage athlete—all four feet, ten inches and ninety pounds of her—that she would have to lose weight if she wanted to make the 1988 U.S. Olympic team. Some people have speculated that this remark was the start of her disordered eating. Christy weighed less than sixty pounds when she died.

Young female athletes are particularly vulnerable to eating disorders when they believe that their performance depends on being thin and world championships are at stake. Gymnasts Cathy Rigby and Nadia Comaneci have also come forward to discuss their battles with eating disorders.

TIME OUT: DOES YOUR COACH KNOW WHAT'S GOOD FOR YOU?

If you are an athlete and your coach pressures you to lose weight in unhealthy ways, don't go along with him or her. Show your coach this book and point out that you believe it would be unhealthy for you to weigh any less than you do now. If your coach won't listen to you, don't just drop the subject. Switch to another sport, or, if you really love the one you're in, talk to another coach, your parents, or a counselor about ways you can continue to participate in your sport while resisting the coach's bad advice.

Remember that your coach probably does not intend to hurt you, but is fixated on winning and needs to learn about the dire consequences of disordered eating and unhealthy weight loss. Speaking up for yourself will keep you safe and may prevent that coach from harming other athletes as well.

woman to develop it in her younger years. However, the combination of disordered eating and amenorrhea puts a young woman, even a teenager or woman in her twenties, at serious risk for loss of bone density. This loss is presently believed to be irreversible. This means that the woman's skeleton, which may not have even finished growing, will never again be as strong as it was before the condition set in. She will be prone to stress fractures and other breaks that aren't even caused by an accident or fall. Far from being a strong athlete, she will be left permanently fragile and severely limited in the activities in which she can participate.

As Loren Mooney reported in *Cornell Magazine,* "Some athletes trim down to a light, but natural, competition weight and improve their performance. Others can cross the fine line to become compulsive about weight loss." The key is finding an ideal weight for performance and health. This is something most adolescents are ill-equipped to do on their own, and it's the reason a well-informed, attentive coach, who demonstrates healthy priorities for his or her team, is crucial to every athlete's success and well-being. The emphasis should always be on maintaining overall wellness.

The bottom line? Work hard to reach your goals, but never risk your health to be number one.

4 Why Anorexia Happens

In her book *Good Enough: When Losing Is Winning, Perfection Becomes Obsession, and Thin Enough Can Never Be Achieved*, Cynthia N. Bitter describes how it feels for an anorexic to look at herself in a mirror:

> *I turned on the light in the tiny hospital bathroom, walked over to the sink and looked down into the white porcelain basin, too afraid to look in the mirror. Too afraid to see what I had done . . . of my own free will. I raised my eyes, slowly, and stared into my face. Oh God, my face! Gaunt, sunken-in eyes. Hollow cheeks; scrawny chicken-neck. Parched yellowish skin that called out for hydration, for nutrition . . . for food. How had this happened? What monster had I become? Okay, I'm scared. I'm scared because it's not getting any better. This merry-go-round won't slow down, or let me get off. I wish I could go back to the*

beginning and start over. But I can't. And I can't stop. Not until I'm thin. Not until my breastbone rests on my backbone, will I be assured that all is safe . . . that I am thin.

While it is true that victims of anorexia are obsessed with thinness, to say that they are therefore vain and self-centered is insensitive and ignorant. Anorexics don't set out to hurt others or to be better than everyone else; they focus on losing weight because they believe that they will never be worthy of love unless they are thin.

This fear is unfounded to begin with, because people who truly love you don't base that love on your appearance. But to make matters even worse, anorexics lose the ability to know what "thin" really is, eventually reaching a point where they see themselves as fat when everyone else who looks at them sees sharply defined cheekbones, elbows, knees, ribs, and collarbones, and even the outline of internal organs showing through the skin.

So, not only are anorexics chasing an ideal that won't bring them happiness but that ideal is continually dropping to ever more unattainable levels. For the anorexic, there will always be "just five more pounds."

HOW DOES IT START?

Anorexia can be triggered by anything or by a combination of factors. It is common for it to set in at a stressful time in the victim's life, such as puberty, the breakup of a relationship, a change of schools, or family problems. It often starts as a diet, but soon the victim finds she can't stop dieting, even after reaching her original goal. The American Anorexia/Bulimia Association points out, "It is worth remembering that an eating disorder is not only a problem but also an attempted solution to a problem. That is, the disorder serves some purpose. Like many other symptoms and apparently maladaptive behaviors, an eating disorder, for all of the problems it creates, is an effort to cope and to communicate."

Some researchers are investigating a possible link between eating disorders and brain chemistry. The National Institute of Mental Health has reported that people with anorexia and certain forms of depression tend to have higher-than-normal levels of cortisol, a hormone released in the brain during times of stress. This excess production of cortisol has been linked to a problem in or near the region of the brain known as the hypothalamus. Another hormone, vasopressin, has also been found in high concentrations in people with eating disorders and is believed to contribute to obsessive behavior such as that seen in anorexics and sufferers of obsessive-compulsive disorder (OCD).

WHAT SOCIETY SAYS

Research has shown that the pressures exerted by society are among the most important factors affecting a young person's self-esteem. Unfortunately, what society says can have an unhealthy impact.

A girl born today has a lot to learn about what society expects of her. By the time she enters kindergarten, she is aware of what "pretty" means, and as she begins to interact with other children, she quickly discovers where she stands in the pecking order of attractiveness. Her parents may already have told her that she is "a little doll," "cute as a button," with "lovely hair" and "big beautiful eyes"—those are the things people tend to say in praise of little girls; in contrast, when people compliment little boys, they usually remark on how strong or smart they are.

Naturally, children love attention and want to please their parents, so they try to live up to these compliments, and in their simple way of seeing things, they equate their parents' love with their own beauty. So if another child tells a young girl that she is ugly, she may be petrified that if this is true, her parents will soon stop loving her.

As she moves through the early grades in school, the young girl becomes ever more aware of how her appearance affects other people. If she is a pretty girl, she may find that boys pay more attention to her and teachers are nicer to her. If she is average or unattractive, the girl will notice that prettier girls get more attention and seem to have it easier in life. Many studies have shown that attractive people are more easily accepted in our society and are believed to be smarter and more successful than their less attractive peers. In most cases these judgments are made subconsciously: the person forms her opinion based on the other person's looks but does not realize

A GIRL'S WORST FEAR

According to an article by Judith Newman in *Redbook*, young girls today are more afraid of becoming fat than they are of nuclear war, cancer, or losing their parents.

it. This is what the saying "Don't judge a book by its cover" means.

By fourth or fifth grade, the girl's personality will have been influenced by her opinion of herself and her perception of how others view her. She may be outgoing or shy based on how her attempts to interact with others have been received. She will probably have developed some insecurities by now—something every adolescent goes through—but how she reacts to her changing body and to others' assessments of her will form the basis of her self-image and will have a dramatic impact on the rest of her life.

As she finishes elementary school and moves on to junior high or high school, the teenage girl will have given a lot of thought to her worth as a person. As she has matured, she may have begun to see that there are things besides looks, including loyalty, generosity, and kindness, that make a person good or bad. Where physical attractiveness fits into her personal list of important traits will have been influenced by her friends and classmates, parents and siblings, teachers and coaches, and by a massive group of people that she has never met: the media.

THE MEDIA MACHINE

"The media" refers to all of the print, radio, and television news organizations in our country, as well as the entertainment industry. It is very unfortunate that journalism and entertainment have merged, because journalism, in its purest form, should be an unbiased, neutral presentation of the facts of a story. But as news organizations began to recognize the value of advertising to finance their operations, the line between simply reporting the news, and reporting it in a way that made their advertisers look good, began to blur.

Now it's sometimes hard to tell whether you're watching a news program or a paid advertisement. Companies with something to sell often buy full-page ads in newspapers and magazines that look just like a news story or feature article. Few sporting events would happen without "sponsors," companies that pay to have their logo prominently displayed in the arena or worn by the players.

A blatant example of this is auto racing, where drivers are coached to wear caps with their sponsor's logo and find a way to say the sponsor's name every time a camera and microphone are put in front of them. Such promotional tactics are also common in movies; when an actor takes a drink of Coke or Pepsi in a movie, it's not because the character prefers it—it's because Coke or Pepsi paid for the right to have their logo displayed in that film.

All of this is incredibly manipulative. Many worthwhile causes would get little attention without corporate sponsorship or the sale of advertising space, but the sponsorship comes with strings attached: when you have a sponsor, you are expected to help your sponsor gain new customers.

The important thing to know as a consumer—and you became a consumer the very first time you asked your parents to buy you something—is the motivation behind all the commercials, magazine and newspaper ads, and prominent displays of brand-name items that you see every day. Most companies don't really care about what is best for you, and they don't know how to make you popular, witty, or pretty; they can't make your life trouble-free. But they want you to think that buying their products will do that for you!

Their goal is to make money. They make money when you buy their products. Therefore, they want you to buy their stuff, whether you need it or not. Some companies don't care that their products could injure you or make you sick—they just want your money. This is what the recent controversy over cigarette companies is all about. In most cases, however, advertisers justify their hard-sell methods with the assertion that buying and using something you don't need won't actually harm you. Other than the bite it takes out of your savings, you might think this is true. But is it?

THE BARBIE EFFECT

Once considered a simple, harmless toy, the Barbie doll is now seen by many people as a dangerous influence on young girls. It may seem like just a doll, but Barbie has become much more than that. When a girl sees Barbie as a representation of an adult woman, she begins to think that that is what she should grow up to be.

If a real five-foot-eight-inch-tall woman had the same proportions as a Barbie doll, her chest would measure thirty-four inches, her waist would be a miniscule sixteen inches, and her hips would measure twenty-nine inches; she would have an unhealthy body-fat level of 12 percent, her head would be much too big for her body, and the exaggerated length and shape of her legs would make it impossible for her to walk!

Nevertheless, many people do believe that looking just like Barbie is an attainable goal. Barbie has blond hair: You can have blond hair (by using hair dye). Barbie has blue eyes: You can have blue eyes (colored contact lenses). Barbie has a tiny waist, full breasts, high cheekbones, and a perfectly toned butt: You too can attempt to have all of these things (with thousands of dollars' worth of plastic surgery). Furthermore, wanting to look just like Barbie is often seen as an admirable goal. Even if parents say otherwise, the huge media machine continues to show us actresses, singers, and models who look a lot like Barbie.

Our society may say that it's great to be yourself and people will love you just the way you are, but its actions say the opposite in a much more powerful way. When a girl finds that she does not measure up to society's ideal, her self-esteem plunges and the door is opened for all sorts of problems, from low grades and unhealthy friendships to severely self-destructive behaviors such as drug and alcohol use, and even psychological illnesses such as eating disorders.

"SIMPLY A SYNONYM FOR SLIM": THE MOCKING OF ANOREXIA

An editorial in *Glamour* magazine's February 1999 issue addressed the "tabloid trend of diagnosing skinny celebrities as sick." The issue became more prominent around that time when Calista Flockhart, star of the popular TV series *Ally McBeal,* was seen at the Emmy Awards in a gown that revealed her extremely thin frame. Catty tabloid articles and jokes began to fly, along with rumors and accusations that Flockhart was anorexic. The *Glamour* writer asked, "Why did her weight loss inspire jokes and gossip, not concern? Would the rumors have been as mean-spirited if she'd been diagnosed with, say, breast cancer?"

"Anorexia has become a joke of a disease," the writer continued. "We use the term to describe any woman who's skinny—whether she's perfectly healthy or possibly sick—and in doing so, we trivialize an illness that is excruciatingly real."

Such mocking can be devastating to true victims of anorexia or other eating disorders, who may feel that they will be laughed at or ridiculed if their condition becomes public knowledge. The *Glamour* writer noted one Florida psychologist's experience with a patient who was extremely upset by a TV interview in which a group of models made a joke of sharing a single strawberry for breakfast. "My patient felt as if the terrible disease she has is a joke to the rest of the world," the psychologist said. "But an eating disorder is an agonizing illness— that fact really is minimized."

5 Getting and Giving Help

If you believe you are anorexic or suspect that a friend or family member may be, it is critically important to get help right away. Studies have shown that those who receive early treatment have a better chance for a full recovery than those whose condition persists for years. Left untreated, anorexia can have irreversible consequences; an estimated one in ten cases are fatal.

One of the most difficult things about treating anorexia is that the victim does not want to change. Anorexia is an emotional illness, and it alters your thinking in many ways. Anorexics believe that being thin is the most important thing in their lives. Often, they see others' attempts to help them as a betrayal or sabotage of their efforts. Many anorexics do not want to stop, even when they see the damage they are doing to their bodies. Others do want to stop but are afraid, because anorexia has become the biggest part of their existence; they are afraid that without it, they will be nothing.

HOW CAN I TELL
IF I HAVE ANOREXIA?

Ask yourself:

- Do I count every calorie I consume, even in chewing gum? Do I meticulously inspect and examine my food for any signs that something is wrong with it?
- Am I happy with myself?
- Do I diet frequently?
- Have I ever used laxatives or diuretics (water pills) in an attempt to lose weight?
- Do I have irregular periods, or none at all?
- Do I skip meals, go without eating for an entire day or more, or "forget" to eat?
- Do I force myself to stick to a strict exercise regimen and feel like a loser if I miss a workout?
- Have I ever made myself throw up after eating?

⊙ Do I believe that being in control of my eating shows others that I am in control of my life?

⊙ Do I feel pressured to get above-average grades and excel at every sport and hobby that I try?

⊙ Do I lie about what I eat?

⊙ Do I know what my ideal weight, by medical standards, should be? If so, do I weigh less, or wish to weigh less, than my ideal weight?

⊙ Do I feel like I would rather die than be fat?

If any of these questions has raised a red flag in your mind, consider talking to a parent, counselor, teacher, coach, or other trusted adult to further explore the possibility that you are suffering from disordered eating.

If you are anorexic, you may feel that the control you have over eating is the only comforting thing in your life. Understandably, you may be afraid to give it up. But please know that when you give up anorexia, you will replace it with many other comforting, healthy, good things that will bring you happiness, not illness.

CAN I FIX THIS MYSELF?

If you believe that you suffer from disordered eating or recognize the symptoms of anorexia in yourself, you've taken the most important step in helping yourself: You've identified the problem. This book is giving you a lot of information about your condition, including the dangerous consequences you will face if you don't find a way to stop it. It has also given you a lot to think about, including why you might have developed this problem. You can find many more books to read in the For Further Reading section at the end of this book; some of these sources might offer information more closely tailored to your individual situation.

If you believe that you are at risk for developing an eating disorder, educate yourself about the dangers of eating disorders. Read everything you can find about disordered eating, and learn as much as you can about good nutrition and healthy exercise. Talk to someone—a counselor, or a survivor of an eating disorder—about the behaviors and problems that put you at risk. Then make positive changes in your eating habits and your exercise routine.

Remember that your self-esteem and body image are very important to your well-being; practice positive self-talk on a regular basis, and surround yourself with positive people who make you feel good about yourself. Speak out against unrealistic media images, and refuse to participate in "body bashing" (negative, critical talk about yourself), even if all of your friends are doing it. Always remember that you are a lovable, worthwhile person no matter what you look like, and anyone who values you only for your looks is not good for you. Celebrate your unique qualities, and encourage your friends to do the same for themselves. You can be a positive force in other people's lives as well.

Helping yourself recover from an eating disorder will be extremely difficult, if not impossible, without professional help. Even if you are able to force yourself to eat, no amount of willpower can erase the emotional issues that led you to anorexia.

If you feel that you might need more help than you can find in books but you aren't ready to talk about it yet, it's okay to wait for a short time until you've thoroughly researched your problem and sorted out for yourself how you want to go about changing it. Then tell your parents or ask another trusted adult for help. However, if you are in immediate danger—if you are not eating, or if you are experiencing any disturbing physical symptoms such as an irregular heartbeat, bleeding, fainting or dizzy spells, excessive tiredness, or pain—don't wait. Tell someone now, and make it clear that you need immediate help. In any case, don't take too long to seek help.

Make a commitment to yourself to ask for help two weeks from today, and use that time to finish this book and check out some more at the library. Also think through how you want to handle your recovery. If you wait longer than two weeks, though, you're procrastinating. Don't allow yourself to ignore this problem and don't think it will just go away on its own—it won't! Give yourself a good, positive pep talk, then build up your courage and get a trusted adult involved.

Whether you choose to tell your parents first is up to you. You could start with a school counselor, a teacher, another relative, or by calling a hotline (see the section entitled Where to Go for Help at the end of the book). The important thing is to start. Below are tips on talking to your parents as well as seeking professional help.

HOW TO TELL YOUR PARENTS

At some point during their teenage years, most people experience tension in their relationship with their parents. This is due in part to the normal letting-go process that accompanies the transition to adulthood. In some ways, teens are self-sufficient and capable of making their own decisions, but in other ways they are still very much in need of their parents' guidance. The difficulty comes in recognizing the difference between a situation you can handle yourself and one with which you need your parents' help. Dealing with an eating disorder is something you can't do alone, but unfortunately, many parents are ill-equipped to help their children with this problem.

Kelsey: "I've been pretending to eat dinner for weeks now. I just push the food around and make it look like I ate some, and my parents never notice. Last night I blew up at my mother because I was so hurt that no one could see how much trouble I'm in. I told them I think I'm anorexic, and they kind of rolled their eyes like I was making it up. I know I need their help. How can I get them to take me seriously?"

If you have an eating disorder, you do need the love and support of your family to help you overcome it. But you also must take some responsibility in helping them to help you. Knowing how they might react to your news will help you to remain calm when you talk to them.

⊙ Anger. It is common and normal for parents to be angry at the situation, at themselves, and unfortunately even at their child when confronted with the news of an eating disorder. If this happens, remind yourself that they are probably most angry with themselves. They may ask questions like "Where did we go wrong?" or "Why are you doing this to us?" This could easily put you on the defensive, but try your best not to get angry yourself.

Since most eating disorders develop at a time of upheaval and change in the life of the sufferer, it is very possible that yours was triggered by a family problem. But now is not the time to place blame. You don't have to give a reason for your problem—just tell them that it exists and that you need their help to overcome it. Give them time to "cool off," then choose a time when everyone is calm and relaxed to talk about how they can help you.

⊙ Sadness. Your parents will probably be very sad for you, for themselves, and for the family in general when you bring them your news. They may cry or apologize for not being better parents. They may even experience a temporary depression and express feelings of hopelessness, saying things like, "Your life is ruined," or "How can we ever get through this?" If they do react this way, you will probably feel overwhelming guilt for causing them grief. But do not allow that guilt to stop you from asking for help.

It may be natural for you to try to take care of your problem on your own to spare your parents the pain of seeing you suffer. But you must resist this impulse. No one's life is perfect, and no child is problem-free: Remember that your parents are there to help you when you need them, no matter how much it may hurt them. Reassure them that you will all get through this and things will be better—your life is not ruined—but for now, you must allow them to share your burden.

⊙ Fear. Another possibility is that your parents will become very frightened. They may even say things like "I can't handle this," or "This is too much for me." Single parents may find helping a child with an eating disorder even more challenging because they have no one to help them work through their own feelings. Consequently, they may turn to their children for the emotional support that a spouse would provide, further burdening the child at an already difficult time.

If this is your situation, remember that you are the child, not the parent: you should not have to shoulder the responsibility of "fixing" this yourself. If your parent or parents seem unable to cope with your problem and are depending on you for emotional support, get another adult involved. A person who cares about you but is not as close to you as your parents is less likely to be paralyzed with fear and may be better able to help you.

⊙ Silence. Many people cannot find the words to express their feelings, so they simply say nothing. If your parents react this way, it does not mean that they don't care or that they don't love you. It could be that they just don't know what to say, or perhaps are afraid that they will say the wrong thing and hurt you.

After you have found the courage to talk to them about your problem, this reaction will probably be very frustrating for you. If you feel you're not getting through face-to-face, try writing them a letter. This will allow you to clarify your thoughts and to say everything you want to say. Also, it will allow them time to absorb your words and to choose exactly what they want to say, or write, in response. In your letter, be sure to explain the ways in which your parents can help you, and ask them to give you a response within a certain amount of time (for example, within three days). Tell them that you know this is difficult for them, but it is a serious problem that won't just go away. You are counting on them to help you.

⊙ Embarrassment. Some people believe in keeping family members' problems within the family and not "airing their dirty laundry" by telling others. If your parents are this way, they might tell you not to discuss your eating disorder with anyone else. They may imply or even say flat-out that you should be ashamed of it, and that if other people find out, they will think less of you.

This attitude is wrong—keeping problems and feelings to yourself is not healthy and expressing them is nothing to be ashamed of. But if your parents feel this way, you will have a hard time convincing them otherwise. As long as you know that an eating disorder is not shameful, you can seek help with a professional and choose not to discuss your problem with neighbors, clergy at your place of worship, or teachers or other school officials. If it enables you to see the doctors, therapists, and other professionals you need to help you begin to recover, you may have to live with your parents' attitude.

However, if your parents forbid you to discuss your problem with anyone *and* they fail to get help for you, then you will have to go against their wishes and take matters into your own hands. An eating disorder is an extremely serious threat to your health; if your parents refuse to help you, you must find someone else who will, like a teacher, school counselor, coach, or even another relative.

Keep in mind, however, that this may only be their first reaction; give them a few days to cool off and approach them again. You may find that they have changed their minds and want to help you.

If days or weeks go by after you've told your parents about your problem and they are still unable to get past their initial reaction, it's time to go to another adult. Telling a trusted guidance counselor, teacher, or doctor would be a good choice. Enlisting the help of another close relative may be an option as well. The important thing is that you find someone to help you. Your wellness is the top priority, and you must do whatever it takes to connect with the people who can help you begin to get better.

HOW TO GET PROFESSIONAL HELP

At various points in your healing process, you may need to enlist the help of a professional with experience in assisting sufferers of disordered eating. Now, you may think that no one can possibly know what this is like for you, and you are right: No one can know exactly what it feels like to be you. But that does not mean that no one can help you.

There are many people who want to help people like you, and they have educated themselves in the facts of your illness and have talked to many others in circumstances similar to yours. While they may not have experienced anorexia themselves, they can empathize with you because they have taken the time to learn about the feelings that you're likely to be feeling and the thoughts you're likely to be thinking. They understand that you may feel frightened and out of control, or that you may feel overwhelming resentment at the people who are meddling in your life. They see their role in your recovery as that of a guide to needed information and a trusted confidant who will listen without judging and advise without dictating.

There are many different types of professionals who can help you. People who work in the mental health field—psychiatrists, psychologists, counselors, and therapists—are trained to be good listeners. They can help you sort out your feelings and find the underlying cause for your disordered eating. Then you can work together to overcome it, to change it if possible (for example, a negative body image) and to deal with it if you can't change it (for example, your parents' divorce). Medical professionals, such as doctors, nutritionists, and dietitians can advise you about how to develop healthy eating habits, including choosing the right foods and getting all the nutrients you need from the foods you eat. People who specialize in fitness, including coaches, trainers, aerobics instructors, and physical therapists are a good source of information if you want to develop a new exercise program or expand on the one you already have. A good fitness expert will emphasize the overall health of your body and will encourage you to set realistic goals in three areas: cardiovascular fitness, strength, and

WHERE CAN I GET HELP?

If you are unsure of where to begin looking for help, a good first step is to call a hotline or visit a Web site that offers referrals in your area.

flexibility. He or she will warn you not to push beyond your body's limits and not to use artificial means such as steroids or supplements other than a simple multivitamin, and will stress the importance of enjoying physical activity while staying safe and not overdoing it. Taken together, the advice of these very different advisors will provide you with a strong knowledge base upon which to build your strong, healthy body.

Finally, since most eating disorders stem from changes in the life of the victim, family counseling is often very helpful in stabilizing the sufferer's environment and educating parents and siblings about what the eating disorder is, why it developed, and how to help the sufferer overcome it.

If you are unsure of where to begin looking for help, a good first step is to call a hotline or visit a Web site that offers referrals in your area. There are many hotline numbers, Web sites, and other service organizations listed in the Where to Go for Help section of this book. The people who answer hotlines are trained to listen to your problems and to give you referrals to professionals in your area who can offer long-term, personalized help. Hotline workers are often volunteers, meaning that they do this work because they want to help people, not just to make money. They are interested in giving you the support and information you need to begin your recovery.

What Will Treatment Be Like?

In reality, recovering from anorexia is not easy. Most treatment plans include more than one element, such as counseling along with nutritional education, and are tailored to the unique needs of the individual

MEDICATION AND EATING DISORDER TREATMENT

Some mental-health professionals use antidepressants as a tool in treating disordered eating. Since a person suffering from an eating disorder often shows signs of depression, it is theorized that treating the depression with drugs such as Prozac, Zoloft, Paxil, or Elavil may also help to alleviate the eating disorder. The drug alone will not bring about a cure. Therapy is needed to work through the emotional problems that led to the eating disorder; however, the drug may allow the patient to get more out of the therapy process.

Not all therapists can prescribe medication: psychiatrists can because they are medical doctors, but psychologists cannot. When seeking treatment, be prepared to decide whether you would be comfortable including the use of an antidepressant in your recovery. If you decide to try it, ask questions about its possible side effects and learn as much as you can about what the drug is expected to do for you.

patient. Since anorexia is a psychological illness that causes physical problems, professionals from both the medical and mental-health fields will be involved in your care.

If you are extremely ill, the first step might be spending some time in a hospital to stabilize your physical condition. If so, you can work out a step-by-step plan for your recovery while you're there; you will probably meet many different people who can help you in planning what to do and in carrying out your plan. Steps in your physical recovery may include visiting your primary care physician or family doctor to assess the damage to your body and how to repair it. If you have also been bulimic at any point, a trip to the dentist is a good idea—have a thorough exam and begin a program to reverse any decay that may have begun as a result of purging. Another element in your physical healing is educating yourself in healthy eating habits. You may be referred to a dietitian or nutritionist for help in learning how to eat well and exercise in moderation to maintain a healthy body.

Your most difficult task will probably be your mental and emotional healing. This side of your recovery will most likely involve some sort of therapy, which may be one-on-one or together with your family members or other recovering anorexics. You may find that a combined approach—some individual sessions with a psychiatrist or psychologist combined with some family counseling, and perhaps some group therapy or participation in a self-help group—will give you a variety of useful insights. Whichever approach will be the most comfortable and effective for you is the best one to use.

There is no predictable time frame for recovery from anorexia, but it is not unusual for an initial treatment plan to last six to twelve months. This may sound overwhelming, especially to people who are used to maintaining strict control over their lives, but it is extremely important to put this investment of time into perspective. Remember that your eating disorder did not pop up overnight; you owe it to yourself to make the investment of time that is needed to regain your health. While you may believe that you can "take care of it" yourself through sheer force of will, please do not shy away from professional help. There are no statistics to tell us how many people have managed to recover from anorexia without any help, but there are thousands of cases in which the victims became more and more ill because they sought treatment only after months or years of believing they could "fix it" themselves.

Remember, They're Human Too

When you seek the services of a professional, whether it's a doctor, therapist, nutrition counselor, or trainer, remember that this person is a fallible human being just like you. Experts can make mistakes, and they can exercise poor judgment. It's okay for you to disagree with them or to question their reasons or sources of information. It is important for you to take an active role in healing yourself, and if someone advises you to do something that you think is wrong or that makes you uncomfortable, speak up. Discuss your discomfort. If the advisor becomes defensive

WHAT IF I'M NOT RICH?

It is true that professional help can be expensive. If you have no insurance, or if your insurance won't cover it and paying for such services is a problem for your family, there are low-cost and free programs to help you. They may be harder to find or may take longer to get into, but don't give up. Remember that overcoming your eating disorder is crucial to your health, so keep trying until you get help.

and demands that you follow his or her orders, consider finding someone else to help you. (It may help to discuss the situation with your parents.) There are extreme cases where a person must be hospitalized and treated against her will to keep her alive, but such situations are rare. In most cases, you will be allowed to have a voice in choosing the course of your treatment, and if you are truly committed to healing, the adults who are helping you should allow you to direct your recovery. If you feel that you are not being heard, speak up, and if you still aren't taken seriously, find someone else to help you.

A FRIEND IN NEED: HELPING OTHERS TO PREVENT OR DEAL WITH AN EATING DISORDER

Cori: "There's this girl who sits with me and my friends at lunch. She only eats bean-sprout sandwiches—one a day, with nothing on it, no mayonnaise, no mustard. Sometimes she doesn't even eat the bread. It looks pretty gross—it took me a while to figure out what the bean sprouts actually were. People make fun of her because she's really quiet and doesn't defend herself, even when they ask her why she's eating worms. I offered her a cookie one time because she was staring at it, but she said no because her mother says she's too fat. I couldn't believe it—she's tiny!"

Often it is hard to know what to say when something like the scenario above occurs. Many people are afraid of saying the wrong thing, but they can't imagine what the right thing to say would be, so they simply say nothing. Think back to a time when you told someone about something hurtful that happened to you and the other person didn't say anything. Did you feel heard? Did you feel that the other person cared about you? Most likely you felt ignored or rejected. The other person may have felt terrible for you, but that sympathy didn't do you any good because he or she couldn't express it.

If you suspect a friend or family member is suffering from anorexia or another eating disorder, find the courage to talk to her about it. It is better to say something in a clumsy way than to remain silent, waiting for the perfect words to come into your head. Similarly, it is better to bring up the subject yourself rather than waiting for her to mention it or for the best possible moment. You *should* try to do it at a time when your friend is calm and not in a hurry to be somewhere or finish something. Some other tips for getting a friend to talk about her eating disorder include:

⊙ Avoid telling your friend that she looks thin. "Tell them they look unhealthy or sick, not thin, because thinness is their goal for controlling their food intake," says Joanne Larsen at her Ask the Dietitian Web site. Remarking on the person's weight may backfire, Larsen notes, because "this attention to weight is interpreted by the anorexic as, 'everyone wants me to be fat.' This soon evolves into a power struggle between the anorexic and her family. The anorexic's attitude is 'I am the one in control and I will show everyone I can lose weight.'"

⊙ Be ready to give your friend factual information about anorexia. It may help to have this book with you; offer to lend it to her.

⊙ Avoid attacking or accusing; use "I" statements instead of "you" state- ments, for example, "I've noticed that you hardly ever eat your lunch. Is there something wrong?" instead of "You never eat, so obviously you are anorexic."

SOME QUESTIONS TO ASK WHEN CHOOSING A THERAPIST

The American Anorexia/Bulimia Association suggests asking the following questions when choosing a therapist to help you toward recovery from an eating disorder:

About the Therapist:

⊙ How did you get involved in treating eating disorders?

⊙ What percentage of your clients have eating disorders?

⊙ How much time will we spend focusing on food, weight, and diet issues?

⊙ Will you allow me to come to an appointment even if I have a relapse (fasting, bingeing/purging, over-exercising, etc.)?

⊙ Do you believe people with eating disorders can be cured, or will I always have this disease?

⊙ What things should I know about you? Why should I see you?

About the Therapy Process:

⊙ How would you describe your approach to therapy?

- What goals will we set?

- Will you involve my family in my recovery?

- Will you monitor my weight and what I eat?

- What can I expect during a session? How long will each session be, and how often will we meet?

- What do I have to accomplish for you to consider me recovered?

- Do you accept my insurance? Do you charge for cancellations?

- What days and hours are you available for appointments? Can I call you between appointments, and if so, is there a charge for that?

Keep in mind that there are a number of possible answers to these questions, and the "right" answer is different for each person. Consider how the therapist answers your questions (what he or she says, as well as his or her willingness to discuss these points) and decide for yourself whether or not you would be comfortable with his or her program.

⊙ Practice "empathic listening." This means listening with just one intention: to understand what your friend is telling you and how she seems to feel about it. Many people make the mistake of using the time during which the other person is talking to think about what they want to say next. The problem with that is that when you're thinking your own thoughts, you can't really pay attention to what your friend is saying! Another element of empathic listening is validating your friend's words and feelings. You can do this by making eye contact, using your body language to show that you are paying attention, responding with small, encouraging words such as "uh-huh" or "I see" or "tell me more," and by resisting the urge to compare yourself to her or talk about similar problems of your own.

⊙ Be ready for rejection. Your friend may not be ready to accept help or to face the reality of her problem. She may even react with denial or anger, or tell you that you could stand to lose some weight too! Try not to take these reactions personally; remember that your friend is suffering a great deal of emotional pain. She may lash out at you for raising the subject, but she isn't really angry with you. Give her time, and eventually she may be able to talk to you about it.

⊙ Finally, offer to help in any way you can, but don't promise to keep it a secret if she refuses to tell a trusted adult. Tell her how dangerous anorexia is to her health, and tell her that you care about her and want to help her help herself. Tell her that you are always willing to listen and that she should feel free to talk to you any time about her eating disorder or any other problem. Reassure her that you will still be her friend regardless of what she does about her problem.

HOW CAN I TELL
IF MY FRIEND HAS ANOREXIA?

You may not be able to tell right away when someone is becoming or has become anorexic. However, there are some signs that you may be able to pick up on if you pay close attention. First, review the questions in the box entitled How Can I Tell If I Have Anorexia? on page 49 and apply them to your friend. Then ask yourself:

⊙ Does she seem to be spending more time alone lately?

⊙ How often do I see her eat? Does she finish her meals?

⊙ Does she talk about her body in a negative way, or compare herself unfavorably to me, other friends, or pictures in magazines?

⊙ Is she proud of losing weight? Does she brag about being smaller than others?

⊙ Does she wear baggy clothes or lots of layers? Does she often complain that she's cold?

⊙ Do the bones in her wrists, ankles, or chest seem more prominent lately?

⊙ Is there something happening in her life that could be causing her emotional pain?

Remember that many people suffer from more than one eating disorder at the same time, so watch for signs of bulimia as well:

⊙ Does she frequently go to the bathroom after a meal?

⊙ Have I ever heard her throwing up?

⊙ Have I ever noticed pills in her purse or bedroom?

⊙ Does she have any physical signs such as cuts on her hands or "chipmunk cheeks"?

If any of these questions have you worried about your friend's well-being, find a gentle, caring way to tell her about your concerns and offer help.

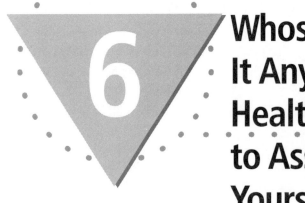

Whose Life Is It Anyway? Healthy Ways to Assert Yourself

If you could do only one thing to avoid problems with disordered eating, what would it be? What do you think is the single most important factor in preventing anorexia, bulimia, and other eating disorders?

While there are always many issues behind each person's eating disorder, the one element that could make the most difference is building self-esteem. This chapter offers some tips on gauging your self-esteem and raising or keeping it high. This chapter also discusses some of the stressful events and milestones that you may encounter as you finish school and move into young adulthood.

For females in our society, one of the most difficult things to do is to separate self-worth from appearance. In fact, some people are never able to do it; they go through life basing their opinion of themselves on their weight or muscularity or skin tone or hair color or any other thing about their bodies that they think others will judge them for. Instead of concentrating on being a better person on the inside, these people feel that they must spend lots of time, effort, and money on what they are on the outside to be loved.

The saddest thing about that is that it's a losing battle: Everyone's body ages and changes, so even if by some miracle you do manage to achieve the physical perfection you've always dreamed of, it won't last. What does last is the work you do to become a wiser, kinder, more generous, more caring person, and once you begin to excel in those areas, you will attract people who are also interested in being wiser, kinder, more generous, and more caring—in other words, you will become more lovable, and so you will be loved even more.

Yeah, but that's not so easy to believe when you have a huge pimple on your nose and your jeans don't fit and the prom is a week away and you're dateless, right? The trick is to break out of thinking from day to day, moment to moment, crisis to crisis, and instead focus on long-term goals. Once you know what you want in life, you can begin to work toward it over time, and things like a bad hair day or a dateless weekend won't seem so important any more. Why? Because you have bigger, more important things to which you can look forward.

But what if you don't know what you want to do with your life? No problem. Having a strong sense of self-worth doesn't mean you have to have your life all planned out. Most high school students don't really know what they want to do with their lives, even though they are experiencing tremendous pressure to commit to something—

THE POWER OF SELF-TALK

People who study self-esteem emphasize the value of positive self-talk. Self-talk refers to the statements you make to yourself, or about yourself to others, regarding your behavior, your performance at some task, your looks, your worth, or any other thing about you. You might not even be aware of doing it, but try to listen to your self-talk. Is it negative or positive? Just about everyone has told themselves they're stupid at one time or another; that is an example of negative self-talk.

Learning to stop negative self-talk and teaching yourself to use positive self-talk is one good way to improve your self-esteem. From now on, work on stopping yourself from saying or thinking things like, "I'm so stupid!" or "Why would anyone want to go out with me?" or "I'll never be able to do this." Instead, learn to be kind and patient with yourself. Tell yourself things like, "I'm not stupid, I just don't get this yet" or "If he doesn't think I'm good enough for him, then he's obviously not good enough for me" or "I know I can do this if I just keep trying." Praising and encouraging yourself is not arrogant or conceited; it's a healthy way to raise your self-esteem, and that will help you to be the type of person you want to be.

career or college or the military or religious life or marriage and kids. Not knowing what you want but feeling pressured to figure it out quickly can be so stressful that it can affect your self-esteem.

The truth is that you can have long-term goals for yourself that don't require the selection of any one path—not yet. First, figure out what your values are, decide what type of person you want to be, and begin working toward becoming that person. Everything you learn about yourself as you develop your own personal moral code will help you to choose a life that will make you happy.

Once you begin to make your self-esteem a priority, you will find that other areas of your life become easier to handle and goals become easier to achieve; often things will seem to just fall into place for you. This does not mean, however, that you will never again have a hard time in life. Everyone has challenges to face. How you react to them will have a lot to do with how you feel about yourself.

This chapter will describe just a few of the challenges you may face in the coming years, along with some ideas on healthy ways to cope with them. As you read in chapter four, times of crisis are often the trigger for an eating disorder; arming yourself with good information before trouble arrives may help you to avoid unhealthy coping mechanisms.

DATING

Janice: "My life was so perfect before Thom broke up with me. I had everything just the *way I wanted it—I always had a date for the weekend and for dances and games, and I felt so special when I went to my locker and found him standing there. Everyone thought we were the perfect couple. Now I just can't seem to get anything done. I wish he would give it another try, but he says he won't. I don't know what to do."*

Romantic relationships are one of life's greatest joys, but they are also the source of many of its sorrows. When your emotions are laid bare for another person to cherish or discard, it can be difficult to keep a strong sense of self-worth.

The truth is, love complicates everything. People make compromises that they swore they never would, give up people and things that were previously very important to them, and do things they thought they never would or could do, all in the name of love. When you're in love, it can be hard to make clear-headed choices. Sadly, many people look back on a time when they were madly in love and berate themselves for being "so blind" or "so stupid." The complex mix of feelings that accompanies a broken relationship quite often leaves your self-esteem (and your pictures of him or her) torn to pieces.

When a breakup happens, give yourself time to grieve for the relationship. You need time to get used to the idea that the two of you won't be together any more. But once you've given yourself that time, move on—don't stay hung up on the past. You have a lot to offer, so don't let a breakup keep you from pursuing your goals.

HOW CAN I CHECK MY SELF-ESTEEM AND BODY IMAGE?

Ask yourself:

⊙ Do I feel inadequate after reading a teen or women's magazine?

⊙ Do I think it's okay for people to be proud of their accomplishments?

⊙ If I had all the money in the world, would I spend it on plastic surgery to enhance my body?

⊙ Do I think anyone can be thin if she just tries hard enough?

⊙ Do I think I'm better than kids who are less attractive than me? Do I think more attractive people are better than me?

⊙ Do I feel unworthy of the attention of older or more popular kids?

⊙ Is there something that's unique about me that I am proud of or glad to have?

- Does anyone ever tell me I'm talented? Smart? Kind? Generous? If so, do I believe it, and if not, do I feel like a loser?

- If I gained fifty pounds as the result of an illness, how would I feel about myself?

- Do I hate trying on clothes because I dislike focusing attention on my body? Do I hide the size tags?

- Can my body do everything I want it to do, like run a mile or catch a ball or do a handstand?

- Do I value my body for what it can do, not just the way it looks?

If any of these questions has caused you to rethink the way you perceive yourself and your body, think of some ways to build up your self-esteem. Practice reminding yourself that your worth as a person does not depend on your appearance, and that no matter what, you deserve happiness, kindness, and respect.

FINISHING SCHOOL

Chris: "I thought I would be so happy once I was out of high school. I couldn't wait till graduation. I guess I just figured everything would come together, and my life would be great. But now it's been a month, and I don't feel any different. Actually, I feel kind of bored and lonely. I don't get to see my friends much, and—I can't believe I'm saying this, but I miss going to class and doing homework. I'm starting college in the fall and I can't wait till this summer is over."

Graduation is, for many people, a bittersweet milestone. It's a happy occasion because it highlights your accomplishments, but it is also sad because you realize that an era of your life is finished and you may never again be with all of the same people in the same place. After high school, you may plan to go on to college or jump right into the working world, either of which may involve moving away from home. You may plan to get married and start a family of your own. All of these changes happening at the same time can be overwhelming and may leave you feeling lost or unprepared for your new obligations. So how do you hold on to your self-esteem when suddenly what's expected of you is very different, and possibly even unclear?

Again, focus on your values. If you can keep in mind the qualities that are important to you—family, honesty, or a strong work ethic—you will find a way to apply them to your new obligations and interests. It is possible to remain true to yourself, even when you're not sure what's happening in your life.

PHYSICAL CHANGES

Monique: "My mother is so obsessed with her looks. I watch how she is, and it's making me dread growing up. I mean, is that all grown-up women do—work on their hair and their makeup and not eat anything and buy fancy underwear that's supposed to make them look thinner? I mean, it's like she hates herself for the way she looks, and she can't stop bringing it up—everyone else can tell how obsessed she is and it makes them uncomfortable, too. If she'd just stop worrying about it, I figure other people wouldn't even notice or care about her appearance, except to tell her when she looks nice."

The ironic thing about trying to make your body into exactly what you want is that bodies are constantly changing. Many people try to escape it, but the fact is that your body will continue to grow and change as you get older. A lot of people find this hard to take.

One of the most common problems people face, and one that is important to the focus of this book, is weight gain. It is normal to gain a small amount of weight gradually as you get older, but many people hate the idea

STAR-POWERED SELF-ESTEEM

Tennis superstar Monica Seles refuses to be a slave to the bathroom scale. She summarizes her healthy philosophy on weight with this thought: "As long as I'm able to move and feel good, it doesn't matter."

and do everything they can to avoid it. Some people go in the other direction and gain too much weight.

It can be difficult to figure out just exactly how much you should weigh. Many factors go into figuring out that "magic number," including the density of your skeleton, your level of activity, your age, your gender, and your height. To make it even more complicated, weight is not the best indicator of fitness—it's your percentage of body fat that counts, and that can't be measured simply by stepping on a scale.

Talk to your doctor, coach, or trainer about the different methods you can use to measure your percentage of body fat. If you are overweight (or, more precisely, overfat), ask him or her to help you make some healthy changes in your exercise and nutrition habits that will result in a leaner you. If you are underweight (or underfat), remember everything you've read in this book—being underweight is unhealthy, just like being overweight, and rather than be proud of it, you should take steps to make your body as healthy and strong as it can be. If you find that you are within your ideal body-fat range, study ways to stay there. Everyone can benefit from learning more about nutrition and exercise.

Remember that there are things you can change about your body—and things that you can't. If you can learn to work on the areas that you can improve and accept the ones you can't, always keeping your health and not just your appearance as your focus, you will be on your way to a healthy body image.

GRIEF

Scott: "My father had a heart attack and died two months ago, and people seem to have forgotten about it already. My friends want me to do stuff, and then they act weird when I say I just don't feel like it. It's like they think I should be over it by now. My mother is trying to hold it together, but I think she feels guilty because they fought all the time anyway, and I think they were going to get a divorce. One time I screamed at her and blamed her for him dying. I still feel really bad about that. But sometimes I just can't help the things that come out of my mouth lately—it's like I can't think before I talk, and sometimes I don't even mean what I say. I feel like I'm losing my mind."

One of the most painful things in life is the loss of a loved one. When someone close to you dies, you feel as if a part of you has died with him or her. You may suddenly find that the mundane, time-consuming daily tasks of your life are pointless—why would anyone spend so much time studying algebra when people are dying? Such feelings of hopelessness are a normal part of grieving, as are physical changes such as a loss of or increase in appetite, excessive sleeping or sleeplessness, anger and hostility, sadness and weeping, or a feeling of numbness that leaves you floating through your days without *really* feeling anything. All of this can add up to feelings of inadequacy, too; you may not see the

AVOIDING "FAT TALK"

Listen to the conversations in any elementary or high-school cafeteria, and you're bound to hear some girls talking about how fat their thighs are, or how much they hate their butts. This "fat talk" is a common bonding experience among young women, but it is unhealthy for their self-esteem. Often members of such groups feel strong pressure to join in with the body-bashing discussions and also to change their eating habits to match what the other girls are doing—even if that means starving themselves.

Think about the ways you and your friends talk about yourselves and each other. Do you engage in negative "fat talk"? If so, speak up and let your friends know that you like yourself just the way you are and that they're fine as they are, too. Practice praising yourself and accepting your body the way it is, and let your friends know that you want them to do the same.

connection between your grief and your lack of motivation in life, and you may start to think of yourself as a loser.

Grieving the loss of someone close to you is a painful process, but it is critical that you do it. Don't think that you need to shove your feelings aside, put on a brave face, and continue to do all the things you were doing before. Everyone needs time to slow down and experience her grief. This may mean that you'll want to spend more time talking to friends, or you may just want to be alone. You may find it difficult to concentrate on your work, or you may welcome the distraction of losing yourself in chores or homework. However it is for you, be gentle with yourself and give yourself a break: take the time you need to cry, or sleep, or just sit and think about the person you've lost. There may be days when you feel great; take advantage of them and get some things accomplished, and don't feel guilty for feeling good when your loved one has just died. There will also be days when you feel terrible and can barely get out of bed; those are the days to take it easy and allow yourself to mourn.

You will eventually work through your grief and reach a point when you are ready to embrace your life fully again. Just make sure to give yourself enough time to get there—don't rush it. Your motivation and your hope for the future will come back eventually. In the meantime, tell yourself that you are busy doing the important work of grieving, and when you're done with that, you'll dive back in to working toward your life's goals.

VICTIMIZATION

Lydia: "I used to think my neighborhood was safe. I was never afraid to walk home by myself or anything. I still can't believe anyone could be so brutal, and all they got was fifteen dollars and my purse. They must have been watching me for a while, because they kept screaming for me to give them my gold chain, but I didn't have it on that day. They said they'll get me the next time I wear it."

Jenny: "I didn't know he was like that, honest. I mean, I thought he was a nice guy, and when he wanted to take me to a movie, I jumped at the chance. After the movie, he wanted to go for a walk down by the water, and I thought that sounded nice, so I went along with it. I didn't know he wanted to have sex, and I told him I didn't want to, but he made me do it anyway. Now I feel used, and my father is acting like it's my fault, and my mother is acting like my life is ruined."

Being the victim of a crime is one of the most devastating things that anyone can experience. Any time someone takes advantage of you, even copying your answers during a test or drinking your parents' liquor, you feel violated. But when the event is a crime such as a mugging, burglary, or rape, you experience a whole new world of painful emotions.

People like to think that they alone are in charge

of what happens to their bodies. It's a comforting thought, and it's one of the reasons that savvy doctors and therapists encourage their patients to make decisions about their treatment rather than just accept whatever they're told to do. People who have been raped, beaten, or robbed lose that secure feeling of being in charge of their bodies. They feel more violated and vulnerable than they ever thought possible, and those feelings don't just go away. In fact, without help, they may never go away: The victim may be left with nothing but all-consuming fear and zero self-esteem.

If you have been the victim of a crime, or of any situation in which you were taken advantage of and left feeling violated, please find someone to talk to. The section at the end of this book entitled Where to Go for Help can guide you to people who can help you work through what happened to you and regain your self-esteem. Remember that you are not to blame for what someone else did to you; it is normal to feel ashamed, but you don't deserve to live the rest of your life feeling that way. With help, you can learn to deal with your feelings and go from being a victim—a person who was the passive, unwilling target of someone else's hostility—to a survivor—a person who experienced an attack and took a proactive approach to healing from it.

SOME FINAL THOUGHTS . . .

Now that you've read this book, you have a strong foundation for building healthy attitudes toward eating, your body image, and your self-esteem. Please share what you've learned with friends, family members, and classmates. Remember to hold your ground against unrealistic societal and media pressure and people who still have uninformed opinions about eating disorders.

If you have lost someone to an eating disorder, visit the Something Fishy Web site on eating disorders and post a tribute to your loved one in the "In Loving Memory" section. Dozens of personal stories appear there, contributed by broken-hearted friends and relatives of eating-disorder victims whose bodies could not withstand the effects of their disease.

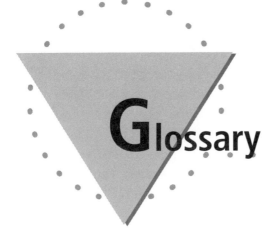

Glossary

alcoholism Psychological and nutritional disease characterized by an inability to resist alcoholic drinks.

amenorrhea Cessation of normal menstrual periods; sometimes caused by excessive weight loss.

antidepressant Drug designed to relieve feelings of depression.

bingeing Eating large amounts of food in one sitting.

bulimia An eating disorder marked by episodes of bingeing and purging.

cardiac arrest When the heart stops beating; can cause death.

cardiovascular Relating to the heart and blood vessels.

disordered Something that doesn't function in the usual way.

diuretic Drug that increases the flow of urine.

laxative A drug or substance that brings on a bowel movement.

logo An identifying mark used by commercial firms for advertising purposes.

malnutrition State of being inadequately nourished, either because of poverty or excessive dieting.

obsession Unwanted preoccupation with an idea or an action.

osteoporosis Condition of loss of bone mass, leading to fragility and ease of fracture.

pathogenic Capable of causing disease.

promotion Actions designed to further the acceptance and sale of goods through advertising or price discounting.

purge To rid the body of food, usually through vomiting, exercise, or laxatives.

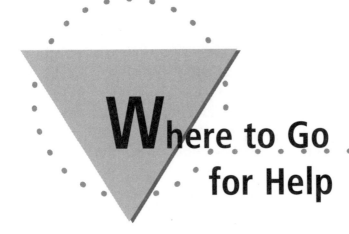

Where to Go for Help

IN THE UNITED STATES

American Anorexia/Bulimia Association, Inc. (AABA)
165 West 46th Street, Suite 1108
New York, NY 10036
(212) 575-6200
Web site: http://members.aol.com/amanbu
Committed to increasing public awareness of eating disorders and providing treatment information and referrals to sufferers and their families and friends.

Anorexia Nervosa and Related Eating Disorders, Inc. (ANRED)
P.O. Box 5102
Eugene, OR 97405
(541) 344-1144

Center for the Study of Anorexia and Bulimia
1841 Broadway, Fourth Floor
New York, NY 10023
(212) 595-3449

Eating Disorders Awareness and Prevention (EDAP)
603 Stewart Street, Suite 803
Seattle, WA 98101
(206) 382-3587
Web site: http://members.aol.com/edapinc
Dedicated to increasing the awareness and prevention of eating disorders. Sponsor of National Eating Disorders Awareness Week every February; provides assistance in organizing local events and educational programs.

National Association of Anorexia Nervosa and Associated Disorders (ANAD)
P.O. Box 7
Highland Park, IL 60035
(847) 831-3438

National Eating Disorders Organization (NEDO)
445 East Grandille Road
Worthington, OH 43085
(918) 481-4044
Web site: http://www.laureate.com/nedointro.html
Provides information on anorexia, bulimia, and binge eating disorder as well as on recovery and treatment.

Overeaters Anonymous
(505) 891-2664
Web site: http://overeaters.org/
Provides information and referrals to local chapters.

Rader Institute Programs
(800) 841-1515
Web site: http://www/raderpro.com/
Offers treatment programs in California, Illinois, and Oklahoma.

Renfrew Center
(800) RENFREW [(800) 736-3739]
Web site: http://www.renfrew.org
Provides information on its treatment centers in the
U.S. as well as general information and referrals.

IN CANADA

Anorexia Nervosa and Bulimia Association (ANAB)
767 Bayridge Drive
P.O. Box 20058
Kingston, Ontario, K7P 1C0
Web site: http://www.ams.queensu.ca/anab/
Canadian organization with 24-hour crisis and
information hotline.

S.A.F.E. (Self Abuse Finally Ends)
(800) DONT-CUT [(800) 366-8288]
Web site: http://www.wwdc.com/safe/
Canadian organization dedicated to reducing the
burden of suffering caused by self-abuse.
Provides information, support, and treatment
programs for victims.

HOTLINES

Boys Town USA
(800) 448-3000
Hearing impaired: (800) 448-1833
24-hour crisis line for girls and boys who need help
with any problem. Parents are also welcome to call.
Spanish-speaking counselors and translation service
for many other languages available.

Bulimia and Self-Help Hotline
(314) 588-1683
24-hour crisis line.

National Mental Health Association Information Center
(800) 969-NMHA [(800) 969-6642]
Provides referrals to local Mental Health Association offices, which can refer you to local programs.

1-800-THERAPIST Network
(800) 843-7274
Provides referrals to local therapists for any condition.

WEB SITES

American Anorexia/Bulimia Association, Inc. (AABA)
Web site: http://www.members.aol.com/amanbu
Contains extensive information on the path to recovery from anorexia, bulimia, and binge eating disorder.

American Psychiatric Association Online: Eating Disorders
Web site: http://www.psych.org/public_info/eating.html
Provides information on anorexia and bulimia, including an extensive section on their possible causes.

Canadian Pediatric Society Adolescent Medicine Committee, "Eating Disorders in Adolescents: Principles of Diagnosis and Treatment"
Web site: http://www.cps.ca/english/statements/AM/am96-04.htm
Article discusses the physical and mental effects of eating disorders and possible barriers to recovery.

Elliott, K.D., BED Confessions
Web site: http://bewell.com/healthy/man/1998/bed/
Contains information on binge eating disorder (BED).

Knowlton, Leslie, Eating Disorders in Males
Web site: http://www.mhsource.com/edu/psytimes/
p950942.html
Discussion of the impact of anorexia and bulimia
on male sufferers.

Larsen, Joanne, Ask the Dietitian
Web site: http://www.dietician.com/bulimia.html
Contains questions about anorexia and answers from
the doctor.

**National Institute of Mental Health:
Eating Disorders**
Web site: http://www.nimh.nih.gov/publicat/eatdis.htm
Contains information on anorexia, bulimia, and
binge eating disorder (BED), and includes discussion of the theorized link between depression and
eating disorders.

Something Fishy
Web site: http://www.something-fishy.org
Huge collection of information, true stories, help
sources, music, remembrances of deceased sufferers, links, and empowering support. Sponsors
live chat events with guests whose lives have been
impacted by eating disorders.

University of Florida Counseling Center, Body
Acceptance and Eating Disorders
Web site: http://www.usfa.ufl.edu/Counsel/text

Contains several scored quizzes as well as information and self-help suggestions.

University of Minnesota Duluth Counseling Services, Eating Disorders Checklist
Web site: http://www.d.umn.edu/hlthserv/counseling/eating_disorder.html
A scored checklist to evaluate yourself for an eating disorder.

For Further Reading

Andersen, Arnold E. *Males with Eating Disorders*. New York: Brunner/Mazel, 1990.

Apostolides, Marianne. *Inner Hunger: A Young Woman's Struggle Through Anorexia and Bulimia*. New York: W.W. Norton & Co., 1998.

Barr, Linda. *Emily's Secret: No One Can Find Out* (fiction). St. Petersburg, FL: Willowisp Press/Pages Press, 1997.

Bitter, Cynthia N. *Good Enough: When Losing Is Winning, Perfection Becomes Obsession, and Thin Enough Can Never Be Achieved* (memoir). Penfield, NY: HopeLines Enterprises, 1998.

Bode, Janet. *Food Fight: A Guide to Eating Disorders for Preteens and Their Parents*. New York: Simon & Schuster, 1997.

Davis, Brangien. *What's Real, What's Ideal: Overcoming a Negative Body Image*. New York: Rosen Publishing Group, 1999.

Duker, Marilyn, and Roger Slade. *Anorexia Nervosa and Bulimia: How to Help*. Bristol, PA: Open University Press, 1988.

Hall, Lindsey, and Monika Ostroff. *Anorexia Nervosa: A Guide to Recovery.* Carlsbad, CA: Gurze Designs&Books, 1998.

Harmon, Dan, and Carol C. Nadelson. *Anorexia Nervosa: Starving for Attention.* Broomall, PA: Chelsea House, 1998.

Hollis, Judi. *Fat Is a Family Affair: A Guide for People with Eating Disorders and Those Who Love Them.* Center City, MN: Hazelden, 1996.

Hornbacher, Marya. *Wasted: A Memoir of Anorexia and Bulimia.* New York: Harper Collins, 1998.

Katherine, Anne. *Anatomy of a Food Addiction: The Brain Chemistry of Overeating.* Carlsbad, CA: Gurze Designs&Books, 1997.

Kolodny, Nancy J. *When Food's a Foe: How You Can Confront and Conquer Your Eating Disorder.* Boston, MA: Little, Brown & Co., 1998.

Krasnow, Michael. *My Life as a Male Anorexic.* Binghamton, NY: Haworth Press, 1996.

Levenkron, Steven. *Treating and Overcoming Anorexia Nervosa.* New York: Warner Books, 1997.

Levine, Michael. *How Schools Can Help Combat Student Eating Disorders: Anorexia Nervosa and Bulimia.* Washington, DC: NEA Professional Library, 1987.

Newman, Leslea. *Fat Chance* (fiction). New York: Paperstar, 1996.

Pipher, Mary. *Reviving Ophelia: Saving the Selves of Adolescent Girls.* New York: Ballantine Books, 1995.

Poulton, Terry. *No Fat Chicks: How Big Business Profits by Making Women Hate Their Bodies—and How to Fight Back.* Secaucus, NJ: Birch Lane Press, 1997.

Prussin, Rebecca, Philip Harvey and Theresa Foy Digeronimo. *Hooked on Exercise: How to Understand and Manage Exercise Addiction.* St. Louis, MO: Fireside, 1992.

Sandbeck, Terence J. *The Deadly Diet: Recovering from Anorexia and Bulimia.* Oakland, CA: New Harbinger Publications, 1993.

Sheppard, Kay. *Food Addiction: The Body Knows.* Deerfield Beach, FL: Health Communications, 1993.

Siegel, Michele, Judith Brisman and Margot Weinshel. *Surviving an Eating Disorder: New Perspectives and Strategies for Families and Friends.* New York: Harper and Row, 1988.

Wolf, Naomi. *The Beauty Myth: How Images of Beauty Are Used Against Women.* New York: Anchor, 1992.

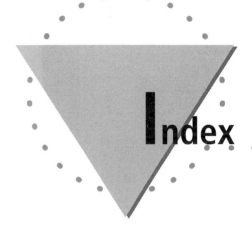

Index

18.95   T80174